THIS BOOK BELONGS TO:

· · · · · · · · · · · · · · · ·

Copyright © Michael Foreman, 2006
The rights of Michael Foreman to be identified as the author and illustrator of this work
have been asserted by him in accordance with the Copyright, Designs and Patents Act, 1988.
First published in Great Britain in 2006 by Andersen Press Ltd, 20 Vauxhall Bridge Road,
London SW1V 2SA. Published in Australia by Random House Australia Pty.,
20 Alfred Street, Milsons Point, Sydney, NSW 2061. All rights reserved.
Colour separated in Switzerland by Photolitho AG, Zürich.
Printed and bound in Singapore by Tien Wah Press.

10   9   8   7   6   5   4   3   2   1

British Library Cataloguing in Publication Data available.

ISBN-10: 1 84270 558 X
ISBN-13: 978 1 84270 558 2

This book has been printed on acid-free paper

Norman's Ark

MICHAEL FOREMAN

Andersen Press • London

Norman is a good little boy who never tells a lie. Honest.
It's just that some people don't believe him. People like his
mum and dad, for instance.

Take last summer, for example. Norman and his mum and
dad went to a safari park for their holiday. They stayed in
a hut like they have in Africa, except the roof wasn't real
straw. It was plastic. But the animals were real. Norman
liked the animals.

In the evenings, Norman was put to bed early, and his mum and dad went to the Safari Bar behind their hut. Norman was happy about this because he could watch TV.
One night there was a terrible storm. Torrential rain rattled on the plastic straw roof and thunder rolled around.

Suddenly Norman heard a noise at the door.
He peeped out of the window and saw a pair of
woolly anteaters huddled up against the door,
sheltering from the rain.

Then a pair of pandas arrived, followed by two aardvarks. They all squidged up together to get out of the rain.

"Lucky they're all quite small," thought Norman.

Then a pair of kangaroos came bounding out of the darkness and, with their big feet and long tails, there was a lot of pressure on the door. Norman could see it beginning to bulge. None of the animals seemed particularly dangerous, so Norman opened the door…

...and they all tumbled in.

But then some really big animals began to turn up.
The hippos were the first. They had to breathe in to squeeze
through the door.

The first rhinoceros managed to get his big horny head into the room, but then got stuck, so the second rhinoceros had to stay outside…with the elephants.

Smaller arrivals, like the koalas, the tapirs and porcupines, managed to scramble through the big rhino's legs. The prickly quills on the porcupine tickled the rhino's tummy and made him giggle, and the hyenas couldn't stop laughing.

The orang-utans and baboons made themselves at home on the sofa.

The sloths went straight to bed…under the bed, that is, because the bed was already full of bears and a pair of buffalo.

The ostriches and emus had a squabble,
the giraffes and grumpy camels
didn't see eye to eye…

and the skunks made a terrible smell in the bathroom.
"But that's the proper place for a smell," decided Norman,
and all things considered, he thought the evening was
going rather well.

Norman was relieved that the jammed rhinoceros in the doorway prevented the lions, leopards and tigers from getting in.

When the rain stopped at last, the animals all said their goodbyes and thank yous to Norman and wandered off into the night, two by two.

Then Norman's mum and dad came home. Now, Norman had done his best to tidy up, but it was a mammoth job. "Where's a good mammoth when you need one?" he thought.

"What's been going on here, Norman?" gasped his mother.
"How did you make all this mess?"
"Oh, I had a little help," said Norman, who always told
    the truth.
        "What help?" demanded his dad.
        "You don't know anyone here."

"Oh, there were anteaters and aardvarks, pandas and porcupines, kangaroos and koalas, armadillos, rhinos, hippos and chimps, hyenas and orang-utans, racoons and reindeer, ostrich and emus, bears and buffalos, and some others I can't remember. Oh, and I think there may still be bats in the bathroom, and I didn't make the smell in there. It was the skunks."

"Is that all?" shouted his father.

"Oh, there were lions and tigers and leopards, but they didn't come in," said Norman.

"Well, we don't believe a word of it," his mum said. "Go straight to bed. We're leaving in the morning, and when we get home we don't want to hear any more of these silly fibs of yours, Norman."

Next morning, when Norman and his parents were leaving the safari park, all the animals lined up, two by two, and waved.
"Bye, bye, Norman," they all shouted, "thanks a lot for last night. And thanks for your address, we'll come and visit soon."

"Norman!" gasped his dad. "I hope you didn't give them our correct address."

"But dad, I couldn't tell a lie," said Norman.

Other books by

MICHAEL FOREMAN

Can't Catch Me!

Cat and Canary

Cat on the Hill

Dinosaur Time

Dolphin Boy
(text by Michael Morpurgo)

Surprise! Surprise!

War and Peas

Wonder Goal